P9-EKY-725

Copyright © 2008 by NordSüd Verlag AG, Zürich, Switzerland.
First published in Switzerland under the title *Beni und das Weihnachtslicht*.
English translation copyright © 2008 by North-South Books Inc., New York.
All rights reserved.
No part of this book may be reproduced or utilized in any form or by any means, electronic or mechanical,
including photo-copying, recording, or any information storage and retrieval system,
without permission in writing from the publisher.

First published in the United States, Great Britain, Canada, Australia, and New Zealand in 2008
by North-South Books Inc., an imprint of NordSüd Verlag AG, Zürich, Switzerland.
Distributed in the United States by North-South Books Inc., New York.

Library of Congress Cataloging-in-Publication Data is available.
ISBN: 978-0-7358-2221-4 (trade edition).
2 4 6 8 10 ✻ 9 7 5 3 1
Printed in Belgium

www.northsouth.com

Little Bunny Finds
CHRISTMAS

PIRKKO VAINIO

NorthSouth

NEW YORK / LONDON

One cold winter evening, on his way through the woods, Little Bunny met four small birds.

"Chick-a-dee-dee-dee! Chick-a-dee-dee-dee!" they chattered.

"Why are you so excited?" asked Little Bunny.

"Don't you know?" said the chickadees. "It's Christmas!"

"What is Christmas?" asked Little Bunny. But the chickadees had already flown away.

While Little Bunny was thinking about this, along came a small deer.

"What is Christmas?" Little Bunny asked the deer.

"Christmas?" said the deer. "I have heard that Christmas is as bright as a shining star."

"As bright as that?" said Little Bunny.
"Then I am going to go find it."
"I will come with you," said Small Deer. And they
set off through the woods to find Christmas.

Before long they met a young wolf.

"What is Christmas?" Little Bunny asked the wolf.

"Christmas," said the wolf, "is as perfect as peace on Earth. That is why I'm not eating you."

"Thank you," said Little Bunny. "Christmas is as perfect as peace on Earth and as bright as a shining star; and we are on our way to find it."

"I'll come too," said Young Wolf. So Little Bunny, Small Deer, and Young Wolf set off through the woods to find Christmas.

Soon they met a wise owl.

"What is Christmas?" Little Bunny asked the owl.

"Ah, Christmas," said the owl. "I have heard that Christmas is as sweet as a mother's love."

"Oh, my!" said Little Bunny. "Christmas is as sweet as a mother's love, and as perfect as peace on Earth, and as bright as a shining star; and we are on our way to find it."

"I will join you," said Wise Owl.

So Little Bunny, Small Deer, Young Wolf, and Wise Owl
set off through the woods to find Christmas.

Little Bunny was in such a hurry now that he forgot to look where he was going. Suddenly he tumbled down a tunnel into a cozy den. He landed right on top of a big bear.

"Excuse me," said Little Bunny. "What is Christmas?"

"Is it a long winter's nap with no interruptions?" grumbled the bear.

"I don't think so," said Little Bunny. "But it is as sweet as a mother's love, and as perfect as peace on Earth, and as bright as a shining star; and we are on our way to find it."

"That is worth getting up for," said Big Bear. "I'll come along."

So Little Bunny, Small Deer, Young Wolf, Wise Owl, and Big
Bear set off through the woods to find Christmas.

At last they came to the end of the woods.
"Look!" shouted Little Bunny. "A shining
star! Christmas must be that way!"

Soon they came to a flock of sheep.

"Is this Christmas?" Little Bunny asked a lamb.

"Maaaa," said the lamb. "Don't be silly. Christmas is down there."

"Is it as sweet as a mother's love, and as perfect as peace on Earth, and as bright as a shining star?" asked Little Bunny.

"It is," said the lamb.

So Little Bunny, Small Deer, Young Wolf, Wise Owl, and
Big Bear walked down into the valley; and there were the
chickadees, outside a stable.

"This must be the place," said Little Bunny.

"Be careful," said Young Wolf.

"Shhh," said Big Bear.

Little Bunny walked up to the doorway. He peeked around the door.

And there was Christmas! As bright as a shining star, as perfect as peace on Earth, as sweet as a mother's love.

"Look!" Small Deer whispered.

"A baby!" Young Wolf sighed.

"Ahhh." Wise Owl nodded.

"Mmmm." Big Bear smiled.

"Happy Christmas," said Little Bunny.